May I Have This Dance?

Port Provident: Holiday Hearts

Kristen Ethridge

Chapter One

"SO, MARTIE, YOU'RE online dating?"

Clair Bell gave the retiree a very puzzled look. Martie Simpson did not seem like the type to swipe left or right...or in any direction, for that matter. In fact, directly over her bed in her studio apartment here at the Port Provident Retirement Community, Martie kept an 11x14 portrait of her being held in her late husband's arms.

Martie laughed. "Oh, Clair, honey, no. I'm just playing games."

Clair didn't realize her eyes could stretch so wide. She could feel the skin in the corners straining to open even larger. "Martie, that's not really smart. The internet is a crazy place. There are so many people who would try to take advantage of you."

"Take advantage of me? Clair, what are you talking about? I'm just playing BuddyWords."

Now Clair felt her eyes narrow until only a mere slit let light in to her pupils. "BuddyWords? The crossword puzzle game?"

Martie's face broke into a grin. "That's the one!"

"So...you're playing an online crossword puzzle game and you used it to invite someone to the May Day dance here at the Retirement Community?"

Clair wanted to understand Martie, she truly did, but this was just downright baffling. When did Martie put down her crochet long enough to learn how to download an app?

"Well, sort of. The person I've been playing with is from here in Port Provident. That's how we started playing together. I met him in the BuddyWords chat room."

Clair clenched her jaw, hoping it would keep her from rolling her eyes. "You met him in the chat room? Okay, so what's his name?"

Martie shrugged. "Bobby0612."

"Martie, that's not a real name. That's a screenname. His last name is not Mr. Oh-Six-One-Two. He could be anyone. He could be a scammer trying to...I don't know...get your Social Security check. I just heard Luke Freiling from CyberCay Security Partners talking about this at the Chamber of Commerce meeting last week."

A loud laugh came straight from Martie's throat. "Then Bobby's a dumb scammer. He can have that piddly little check."

"You know what I mean, though, Martie." Clair found it hard to believe that Martie seemed to think that *Clair* was the crazy one.

"I do." The older woman's gray bun flopped ever-so-slightly on the top of her head as she nodded. "But I've lived long enough wishing for things to be different. I've lived a long time without my Ray. And with my kids away living their own lives in other states, well, I've lived a long time being alone. I'm tired, Clair. You do a great job of planning activities here and making sure we're all looked after. No one could do a better job of running a place like this than you do—there are so many horror stories out there of homes that treat their residents badly. You don't do that, and I know you never will. And I've got friends here—I don't mean that I'm lonely. I just want a little fun. You know?"

Clair raised her arm and patted Martie on the shoulder.

All of Clair's residents had a special home in her heart, but Martie Simpson occupied the penthouse. She loved the dear little woman who was always quoting her favorite Bible verses, telling stories from the war, and gifting hand-made afghan blankets to every new resident. Martie was like the grandmother Clair always dreamed of having.

"I think I do, Martie."

"I know you do, Honey." Martie stared Clair down with love in her gaze. "It wouldn't hurt you to decide to have some fun, too. I said you're great at your job—and you are—but there's a big world outside these walls, you know."

Clair waved at Ellis Lawson as his daughter signed him out for the afternoon. "Be good, Ellis—I'll see you back in a bit."

"See? Even Ellis gets out there. He told me Felicia was taking him to Island Bowl today."

If Clair hadn't known better, she'd say there was more than a hint of *I-told-you-so* in Martie's voice.

"I haven't been bowling since high school." The memories came as swiftly as a shiny ball rolling down the lane. Her long-ago ex-boyfriend Rob had talked her into joining a league at Island Bowl. He said he was in in it for the chance to have his own monogrammed bowling shirt. He'd always made her laugh.

Until the day that he made her cry.

But that was a long time ago. She had worked hard to stop letting the memories of Rob Landers affect her.

And she didn't intend to change her constant desire to keep the past in the past.

Martie had dragged up enough crazy with this BuddyWords May Day date thing. Clair was absolutely not going to let Martie inadvertently pull up anything else that needed to be, metaphorically speaking, left at the bottom of the Gulf of Mexico.

It seemed crazy to lead the conversation back to this BuddyWords nonsense, but it didn't take much for Clair to realize that was a much safer place for her mind to be than dancing around memories of her high school sweetheart.

"So, Mr. Oh-Six-One-Two is going to come here and be your date to the May Day Dance we're putting on next weekend?"

Martie shook her head strongly enough that this time, her bun did a full cha-cha. "No, not exactly."

Clair threw her hands in the air. "Then I'm really confused, Martie. I thought that's what you said."

"I did." She nodded again. "But he's also coming tonight to dinner. He's here in town visiting family. It's his first time back in Port Provident in almost ten years, he said."

"He's coming to dinner here? With you?"

Martie smiled. "Yes. It's lasagna night. He said he loves lasagna. It was a bonus word two weeks ago. We started talking about it. I thought it would be fun to meet him in person."

"Martha Jane Sidwell Simpson, you've gone plumb crazy. I think you need a chaperone."

"Nope. There are two hundred and twelve residents here. I'll be fine." She made a dusting motion with her hands as if to signal that was that to Clair. "Now, if you'll excuse me, I need a little beauty nap before dinner."

She gave a grin to Clair, then turned away and walked down the hall without another word.

When Clair told people that she managed activities and recreation for the local retirement center, most of them assumed that her days were spent calling bingo and bocce ball tournaments. They figured it was a slow, sedate job.

They'd never met Martie Simpson. Or the other two hundred and eleven people who called this cluster of red brick buildings near the seashore home.

Nothing about the Port Provident Retirement Community was dull. It was why Clair preferred to spend her time at work. Her own life paled in comparison. Retirees who'd seen everything and done everything still had more excitement in their lives than a woman who had her whole life ahead of her.

She'd be reminded once again of that tonight when she popped in the center's restaurant to check on Martie. Clair wouldn't be on a first date, herself. She never went on first dates. Even though Martie insisted it wasn't a date, Clair could make sure Martie had a good time—and a safe time.

And somehow, Clair would find a way to tell herself that what she had now was enough.

IT FELT GOOD TO BE home.

Rob Landers looked at all the shops and restaurants and other businesses that crowded along the last strip of land before the water—Gulfview Boulevard. So many of them were familiar. Even in the ten years he'd been gone, they'd remained.

He took a deep breath, processing the emotion of seeing his hometown again for the first time in so long. He wished that, like the long-term establishments, he'd been able to stay. But it wasn't meant to be. His old man had needed help and his mom needed a clean break and getting out of town was the only way to make both of those happen.

Still, reconnecting with Port Provident the last few months had done his soul some good. He'd plugged into some groups on FaceSpace online, purchased a digital subscription to the online paper, and even met someone from the island while playing BuddyWords on breaks at work.

He wanted to know if finding his roots could cure the restlessness that had crept under his skin.

If any place could show him the way, it would be Port Provident.

As Rob slowed down at the stop light, he looked to his left, taking in more of the local landscape.

THERE IT WAS. Island Bowl. Man, he'd spent so many hours there. He'd spent so many hours *with Clair* there.

Clair Bell. He'd never forgotten the honey-blonde girl who'd been his first love. But he knew she'd forgotten him. In this whole crazy pursuit of his past, Rob knew without a doubt that the roots that had once connected him to Clair were now shriveled up and dead.

Just like the addiction that chased his pop off the island.

Just like the angry divorce that meant he needed to be separated from his mother and sister.

Just like the freedom and happiness he'd once known while roaming the halls of Port Provident High School.

Just like so many things in his life.

Rob was done with bitter ends and loss.

This trip to Port Provident was about finding himself and giving himself the chance to see how his life could have been different. It was about reconnecting with people and places that had once meant a great deal in his life.

It wasn't about regret. And every memory he had of Clair Bell was wrapped in a cloud of regret. Rob turned his head away from Island Bowl and waited for the light to change from red to green.

Somehow, these few seconds spoke to him deep inside. They were the perfect picture of everything he was trying to do. He was trying not to look at the things in the past that had hurt him—but instead, he was waiting for the sign that he could move forward.

It wasn't long before he saw the sign he'd been looking for—at least for tonight. The Port Provident Retirement Community. He'd met LongTimeMartie online in a forum for people who played an app-based crossword puzzle game called BuddyWords. They struck up a friendship after realizing they had Port Provident in common. When she found out that he was coming to town to see family, she invited him to lasagna night at her retirement home.

His sister Gretel almost laughed herself off the side of her dolphin tour boat when she heard about his plans for dinner.

"She seems like she needs a friend, Gretel. Her daughter just moved to Ohio with her family, but she stayed behind. Now she's all alone on the island. I know what that feels like. You do too." Rob remembered their conversation from the night before.

"Yeah, I do. I wonder if some knight in shining armor will show up for me when I go to a home someday," Gretel mused.

"I'm no knight. And if I had armor, I'm pretty sure it would be tarnished," Rob told his cousin.

He looked on the passenger seat next to him. He'd bought a dozen roses in a variety of colors. He was no white knight, but he knew that to *have* a friend, you first had to *be* a friend. And this trip to Port Provident was all about being a better version of himself and putting together the pieces of the puzzle to help him start over and become who he'd always hoped he could be.

Rob walked in the door to the facility. A tiny woman with a loosely wound gray bun smiled broadly. "Bobby?"

"LongTimeMartie?"

Her smile became even brighter. He held out the multi-colored blooms. She leaned close and inhaled deeply.

"What a sweet young man you are, Bobby."

He cleared his throat a bit. "I actually go by Rob. Bobby was my nickname when I was a kid. My username is my kid nickname and my birthday. Bobby0612...my birthday's June 12."

"Oh, how cute," the older woman said. "Bet you can't guess how I got mine."

"I'm afraid I can't." There were too many possibilities, and not a one of them seemed like something he wanted to say out loud to a woman old enough to be his grandmother.

Martie took the bouquet from Rob. "It's from my favorite song. *It's Been a Long, Long Time* by Harry James and his Orchestra from back in the World War II days. My husband and I danced to it the night before he shipped out to Europe. It was our song."

Her explanation brought a smile to his face. "It must be nice to have true love like that."

She closed her eyes. "Oh, it was. I miss him."

"So, he's not here with you?" Rob didn't quite know what else to say.

"Oh, he's always with me," she said, tapping her finger over her heart. "Right in here. Now, let's get to the dining room before Mary Ellen gets the good table. I want to make sure we're sitting right in the center so everyone knows this old girl still has some fun."

CLAIR TRIED TO BE STEALTHY. Although she often worked late and walked around the restaurant area chatting with residents, she felt way too much like a chaperone right now.

Play it cool, Clair Bear. Just play it cool.

Just as she expected, Martie had chosen the table right in the center of the room. It was exactly like her to make sure everyone saw her and that she saw everyone. Martie was hardly ever subtle, and Clair loved her for it.

Everything seemed to be going well. There were two glasses of tea, a basket of bread, two salad plates heaped with spring mix and croutons...and Rob Landers.

Suddenly, nothing was cool.

Everything flipped around like a salad being tossed in a big, wooden bowl.

Why was Martie having dinner with Rob?

Why was Rob even in Port Provident? Clair choked on a little bit of bile. He left. He left in the middle of the night without saying goodbye. He never reached out again. And to her knowledge, he hadn't been back in ten years.

Bobby0612. The twelfth of June. That was his birthday. And his mother used to call him Bobby, even though everyone else called him Rob. Clair wanted to kick herself for not figuring out the user name.

She tried taking a steadying breath, refusing to give into the urge to condemn herself. After all, there were a lot of guys named Bobby in this world. How was she supposed to know that the one who'd broken her heart and actually went by Rob liked to play word games on his phone?

Clair figured all he knew how to do was play mind games.

And heart games.

He'd played her back then. Just like a game.

When Martie's daughter moved up north, Clair promised that she and the rest of the staff would take good care of Martie. And that meant there was no way that she was going to let Rob Landers spend any more time with the retiree. Not even on that silly crossword game. She'd warned Martie about crazy people who wanted to scam retirees out of their life savings.

It wasn't exactly dollars and cents, but Rob had scammed Clair's heart back in high school and run off, leaving it just as empty as any cleaned-out bank account. She knew who Rob Landers was and how he worked, and she was not going to let him anywhere near Martie or any of the other retirees under her watch.

Nope.

Clair was older and wiser. And scared stiff. How could she say anything to Rob after all this time?

She marched across the dining room. She had six more steps to figure out what she was going to do.

"Martie?" Clair stopped short of the table and crooked her finger. "Can I have a word or two with you for a minute?"

Martie's face lit up like a strand of lights surrounding a Christmas tree. "Of course, darling. But first, I want you to meet my new friend. This is Rob Landers, the real-life Bobby0612. Rob, this is Clair Bell. She's our activities director here. She's like another granddaughter to me."

Clair got a great deal of satisfaction out of watching Rob's complexion drop several shades until it bottomed out somewhere between puke green and ashy gray.

"You work here?"

"This is my home. These are my people." She crossed her arms, hoping to deflect any bad ju-ju that seeing him might stir up. Childish, yes. And the fact that she even so much as thought the words *bad ju-ju* made her roll her eyes at her own ridiculousness. But still...

"Wait, so you live here?"

She stared him down. It was way more fun than it should have been to watch him squirm. "*I* never left."

"Clair, honey, you sound mad. Do you two know each other?"

"Yes," Rob choked out.

"Not really," Claire said with a confidence fueled by the pallor in Rob's face.

Martie laid her fork on the side of her salad bowl. All eyes in the restaurant had turned toward the center table. They'd be talking about this confrontation for days over bingo.

"Clair—do you know him or not?"

Clair decided that honesty was the best policy. "I thought I did. Once. But no, apparently I really didn't."

"So how do you know each other?" Martie continued to dig.

"School." Clair focused on keeping it short.

Unfortunately, Rob had not gotten the same memo. He dove in at the same time as Clair, but gave more of an explanation than she ever wanted her residents to know. "We dated for two years in high school. I haven't seen her since I moved."

Clair stood silent.

"So...*you're* the one who got away?" Martie began to hum something that sounded suspiciously like a big band tune.

"What are you singing, Martie?"

Martie smiled. "Oh, just my favorite little song. *It's Been a Long, Long Time.*"

Clair couldn't even twitch. She was frozen. She knew the lyrics to that song. She did not want Rob to kiss her once or twice or once again.

Never again seemed far more appropriate.

"It has been a long time," Clair said. She lowered her voice slightly. "But not nearly long enough."

Martie swallowed, then yawned with a big stretch. She pushed the chair back, then stood up. "My goodness, speaking of long, it has been a looong day. And you know what they say about elderly people needing their rest. Rob, I'm so sorry, but I've got to go back to my room. Right now. Really nice meeting you."

For the first time in more than a decade, Clair looked at Rob and saw her own expression mirrored in his dark eyes. The look on his face held the same amount of shock and disbelief as she knew her own features did. Martie scampered out of the room with a rate of speed that belied the number of arthritis pills she took on a daily basis.

Rob took a deep breath and pointed at the now-vacant chair. "Do you still like lasagna?"

Chapter Two

CLAIR'S FIXED STARE cut him deeper than any razor blade or knife he'd ever known. Rob felt pretty certain that there were machetes out there that would seem dull in comparison to the look Clair threw down just now.

She just stood, unmoving. Unanswering. And her gaze remained unwavering.

"Lasagna, Clair? Would you like to join me?" He felt ridiculous asking. Her answer was painted clearly across the angles and curves of her face.

But everyone was staring. Someone had to make the move.

And since Clair resembled a stone monolith, it was clearly going to have to be him.

She clenched her jaw in reply. "Not really."

Her voice sounded low, and each short syllable had been measured precisely, like an ingredient in a dish.

"I can see that." Rob toned his voice down to her volume. "But everyone is staring. You might want to just pretend."

Clair's head turned slightly to the left, then slightly to the right. She took a deep breath and slowly sank into the chair Martie vacated. A muscle at the far back corner of her cheek continued to twitch and fire, leaving no doubt about her true feelings.

"So, um...you work here?" Small talk seemed like the best option until everyone surrounding the central table took their focus back to their own plates.

Rob thought Clair nodded, but he wasn't sure.

"I do."

"Been here long?"

"Six years."

"So, I guess college and then here?"

To say this felt uncomfortable was something like calling a blistering sunburn a minor scratch. This one was going to itch for a long time.

Actually, it had itched for about a decade. But when it came to Clair Bell, Rob had never given himself permission to scratch that itch—or even acknowledge it. Because he knew that once he started thinking about Clair, he'd never be able to stop.

It had been best to keep everything about Clair—and the relationship they'd had back when everything was fresh and bright and new—locked in a box.

Looking at Clair made him wish he'd never come back to Port Provident. He came back with good intentions to reconnect with the people he'd loved. But Clair—Clair, he'd loved in a different way. He'd loved her with his whole heart. And he'd never be able to get that back.

For now, however, he was stuck sitting across a small, round table with a white tablecloth from the girl he'd once planned a future with. Only now, she was a grown woman. But nothing had changed. Her blonde curls still fell across her shoulders. Her eyes remained the color of the butterscotch in his great-grandmother's antique candy jar.

Rob wondered if her smile still seemed just a little too big for her face.

He shrugged, figuring that he wouldn't discover the answer to that question tonight. There was no way anything he said or did would make Clair Bell smile. Not now. Not ever again.

"What?" Her voice probed.

Rob sat a little straighter in the wooden chair. "What?"

"You shrugged. Is something wrong?"

Might as well answer honestly. It couldn't possibly make things any more awkward than the current situation. "Well, maybe just a little."

Her eyebrows shot straight up toward her hairline. "Really, Rob? How do you think I feel? Everyone here has seen this whole thing. I have to come back in to work tomorrow. How many times do you think I'm going to get asked who you are and how do I know you? I don't even know how I would begin to reply."

She placed her hands in her lap and stared down at them. Suddenly, Rob didn't see spitfire and brimstone in front of him. He saw vulnerability.

And hurt.

Hurt that he'd put there, just as sure as if he'd laid bricks in a wall and sealed them together with mortar.

"Come on," he said. "Let's go."

Clair's head bobbed up. "What? Where?"

"Anywhere but here. You probably have a few things you want to say—or yell—at me, and you're not going to be able to do it in the middle of this dining room."

"YOU SHOULDN'T BE HERE."

The lights of the parking lot glowed a soft orange-yellow in the dim of the early spring evening.

Clair tried to choke down the words she really wanted to say. It had been hard enough to maintain her composure in the dining room, but out here, it wasn't a question of composure. It was a question of not losing it entirely.

"I didn't know you'd be here, Clair. Honestly. I was just trying to brighten a little old lady's day. Martie seems lonely."

"She misses her kids and her grandkids. It's hard when the people you love go away and you don't hear from them like you used to." She raised her eyes and met his straight on. "Or at all."

Rob took a step back and raked his hand through his hair. "Fair enough."

"So, where have you been?"

"South Carolina." He answered slowly. Clair couldn't tell if Rob was holding something back. But she'd already opened this line of dialogue. She decided to finish what she started.

"*Carpe momentum*," she muttered.

"Seize the moment?" Rob questioned.

Clair could feel the smirk sweep across her face. "It's past dinner time. I can't very well seize the day right now."

Rob stuck his hands in his pockets and leaned against the light pole. "That's fair."

"Nothing about this is fair." A thick tendril of depression wrapped around her heart and squeezed. No, not this. Not again. Clair didn't want to give in, but once the feeling found an opening and reached out those powerful claws, there was little Clair could do.

She knew this song and dance very well.

She'd been battling depression for too many years. And so much of it was tied up in the man standing in front of her. The gray clouds had followed her from her early teenage years. But the darkest days of her life were the ones after Rob went away. They lasted for years and made her question everything about herself and wonder if she even wanted to keep putting one foot in front of the other.

Some days, she couldn't even put one foot out of bed. Clinical depression was like that. And it was Clair's constant companion, a whisper of smoke and fog that followed her always, like an unwelcome shadow.

"I didn't mean it like it sounded, Clair. If you want me to leave, I will."

Clair wanted to physically push him away, wanted to force him to go. It felt important to her that he should know how strongly she felt about hoping he'd honor the offer he'd just made.

But more than that, she desired to achieve the goal that had been out of arm's reach for so long. She wanted to beat depression. She wanted to be free from the what-ifs and the things that haunted her. She knew that there was no one thing that Rob could say that would be a magic switch. There was no one thing that would make it all go away.

But maybe, just maybe, if she could ask some questions and get some answers...maybe she could start on the road to healing the regrets that she knew held her back.

"I don't want you to leave," she said quietly. The sound of cars driving along Gulfview Boulevard almost drowned her out.

"So...you want me to stay? Out here? In the parking lot?"

No, that wasn't it either. She had to do this right. It could be her only shot to jump-start her recovery in this area that had affected her so much and made her feel powerless in her own skin.

"Could we maybe meet up somewhere while you're here?" She felt the pinprick of ice shaking through her veins. The chilly pulse made her both hyper-aware of the situation and terrified of it at the same time.

Clair swallowed hard as she waited for Rob's answer.

"Sure." His voice came across flatly, but the nod of his head reassured her. She'd seen him give that casual stamp of approval hundreds of times before. "Do you have any time tomorrow? I don't have a lot that's written in stone while I'm here, so I can make something work on your schedule."

"I get off at five."

"Where would you like to meet?"

Would it be better to be in a public place so there'd be plenty of noise and distraction? Or should she set up the meeting in an environment she had more control over? Clair weighed the options in her mind.

She didn't want to go somewhere that held memories of their past, so that ruled out a number of the local restaurants and many other locations on the island. Clair took a deep breath. She needed to get this one right.

Maybe control was the way to go. A home court advantage, so to speak.

"I live in a little cottage at the back of the property here. Maybe five-thirty tomorrow?" Clair tried not to choke as she swallowed hard.

There was so much risk in inviting Rob to her home, her sanctuary. But she knew she needed to have the upper hand. She needed to be some place she felt comfortable.

"That will work. Should I bring anything?" He seemed just as hesitant as she felt.

Clair's internal dialogue scolded herself for even noticing. This wasn't going to be about Rob—even if he tried to make it so. This would be about Clair. About questions, answers, closure...and the road to healing she'd searched for down so many paths for so many years.

This would be about the future.

Her future.

"Just bring honesty."

"SHE'S A GOOD GIRL." Martie pushed her walker along the sidewalk atop the high wall that hugged the Gulf of Mexico and provided the southernmost border for Port Provident.

Cars swooshed by, going to-and-fro on Gulfview Boulevard, but Martie paid them no mind.

"If I'd known you two had a history like that, I wouldn't have invited you to dinner, Rob."

Rob nodded. "If I'd known she worked at the retirement community where you live, I wouldn't have come to dinner."

"But she does. And you did." Martie pursed her lips. Rob watched the train of thought criss-cross the older woman's face.

"I did. And now she wants to meet up to hash it all out. 'Bring honesty,' she said. Martie, I haven't been around her since we were teenagers. You know her better than I do now. What do I do? I messed it all up when I left. I saw pain in her eyes yesterday and I put it there—even though it was years ago. I don't want to cause her more pain today. That's not who I am. But I honestly don't know what to do. It's almost like walking on glass."

Martie stopped at a bench. She scooted her walker around and then sat down, facing the water. She patted the space next to her. "Have a seat, young man."

Rob did as he was told.

"What do you wish you'd done differently back then?"

Rob closed his eyes, feeling the tension at the base of his skull as he flexed his neck backwards.

"Everything."

He'd been so desperate to fix his dad's problems that he had been completely unaware of the mess being left behind. That's what this trip was for. He promised himself he'd restore his relationships with his mom and his sister.

But Clair?

Clair had never been in the plan.

There were no answers. There were no answers because there was only one question: would there ever be a time when he stopped loving the girl who stole his heart at fifteen?

Actually, he was wrong.

There *was* an answer.

And it was no.

No, there would never be a time when the thought of Clair Bell didn't make his chest tighten as though in a vise. There would never be a time when the thought of Clair Bell didn't lead to a million other thoughts of what was, what could have been, and what should have been different.

Everything felt like the perfect answer to Martie's question. Because *everything* should have been different.

"How do you undo everything you did wrong?" he muttered to the wind.

Martie looked squarely in Rob's direction. He could feel her stare boring into the side of his face. "Well...just like the elephant."

He remembered that as his own grandmother aged, she started making less sense. Clearly, the same thing was happening to Martie.

"Elephant?"

"The elephant." She nodded with conviction. "And how do you eat one?"

Oh...now he followed her train of thought. "One bite at a time."

"Exactly, my boy. And that's exactly how you start to make amends with Clair. One step at a time. One action at a time. You can't undo everything at once, so don't even try. You'll scare her to death. Earn her trust one step at a time. There's a proverb in the Bible about trust. Have you heard of it?"

Rob felt the corner of his mouth twist. He hadn't set foot in a church in a long time. Like probably before he learned to read. "No, Martie, I haven't done much Bible study."

"You should." Her words held the same note of conviction he'd heard just moments ago. "There are a lot of good life lessons in Proverbs. Things anyone can benefit from. Anyway, Proverbs 28:25 says 'selfishness only causes trouble—you are much better off to trust the Lord.' That's my advice to you. Leave the selfishness behind. Trust and pray."

A bubble pushed at the center of Rob's chest. There was just...nothing there. Martie sounded confident in what she had recommended.

But Rob knew it wasn't for him.

He wasn't the praying type.

He just wasn't.

He knew it worked for lots of folks. Clearly Martie put a fair amount of stock in it. But it wasn't for him.

God had given up on guys from broken homes with broken dreams like him.

And it was okay. Rob understood.

He'd given up on his own dreams a long time ago, too.

Chapter Three

"I'M NOT READY FOR THIS," Clair said out loud, although there was no one around to hear.

The flicker of the blue flame on the gas stove mirrored the twitchy anticipation pulsing in Clair's veins. She brought a pot of water to boil on the back burner, staring at the surface of the liquid, fading into some form of kitchen-induced self-hypnosis as she waited for the little bubbles to begin floating up.

Waiting.

That's all she'd done for years. Her life had taken on a distinct holding pattern.

Clair sucked in a deep breath. She needed to listen to the advice her counselor had given her for years. Reframe things into a positive.

"I'm *positive* that I'm not ready for this."

One bubble pricked the surface of the water. As she watched, Clair began to see a parallel between the stock pot and her own evening. Ready or not, when the time came, it would all happen.

She needed to change her attitude. Being positively not ready was just like riding a bullet train to disaster town. She'd walk away from the evening with a strong urge to hide and never get out of bed again. And that was no longer acceptable.

Depression would no longer run her life.

Tonight was about closure.

Tonight was about healing.

Tonight was about all those dreams she'd dreamed and never had the chance to allow to come to fruition.

Tonight was about closing out those memories so she could start dreaming again.

After they talked, Rob would walk out the door again. And this time, she knew it—and was looking forward to it.

But first, she needed to get through it.

A knock sounded at the door. Clair pulled in another deep breath of steadying oxygen as she walked toward the front of the house. It filled her mind and the blood that swished through her body, giving her the air she needed to take the step that would eventually lead to the freedom she sought.

She could do this.

She was *positive* she could do this.

Clair laid one hand on the door knob. She gripped it, feeling the cold of the metal cylinder under the tips of her fingers. She wiped her other hand down the front of her pants, trying to rid herself of any traces of nervousness. She didn't want Rob to suspect she was anything other than completely in control tonight.

If she could fool him, then she had a better shot of fooling herself.

Fake it 'til ya make it, she often told her residents when they tried something new. It was time to take her own advice.

She turned the knob and pulled open the door. "Hey, Rob. Thanks for coming."

Clair hoped the smile she rigged up on her face looked sincere.

"Clair. Thanks for giving me the chance to come over and talk."

She wiped her hands down the front of her dark jeans one more time for good measure. "Sure. I think it's a good idea, don't you?"

Slowly, she closed the door behind Rob. "I just put on some water to make pasta. Do you still like spaghetti?"

Rob nodded. "My food choices still resemble those of your average ten-year-old, so spaghetti definitely qualifies."

Yet another thing that hadn't changed. Rob seemed like the same guy she'd known years ago. Maybe she was the only one who had become a different person inside. "So...I guess I don't need to bother fixing a salad?"

He shook his head with a laugh. "Not really, unless you want one for yourself."

Clair opened the box of pasta and poured it in the water, which had now come to a rolling boil. "Do you eat any vegetables?"

"Of course," Rob said with a short laugh. "Carrots. With Ranch."

She threw him a glance over her shoulder. "Ranch isn't a vegetable."

"Nope," he agreed. "It's a vehicle. It makes vegetables edible. It's one of the greatest inventions of all time."

She gave the water and pasta a quick stir, then adjusted the temperature. "So right up there with the Gutenberg press and Cyrus McCormick's harvester?"

His head tilted slightly as his shoulders gave a knowing shrug. "Basically."

The kitchen grew quiet as they each ran out of highlights of dressing and inventions to speak of.

"How long have you lived here?" Rob looked around the small apartment.

Clair walked to the fridge and pulled out a pitcher of tea and a bag of mini-carrots. "About two years ago when I got my promotion. It's nice to not have to commute, and I do have great neighbors. They look out for me."

Rob folded his arms across his chest. "They do. Martie thinks you've hung the moon."

"Aww, that's sweet. I love her. She's got so much love in her heart. I think with her family being gone, she's just looking for an outlet. She's a giver."

"She really seems like it. Is it okay if I sit down?" He pointed at the white wooden chairs arranged around the small butcher block-style table.

"Of course. Please." Clair reminded herself to calm her frayed nerves and treat Rob like any other guest. "Would you like a glass of iced tea?"

"Sure. That sounds great."

As Clair pulled two glasses out of the cabinet, she tried to keep the conversation going. Small talk seemed like a good place to start for the evening. "Martie said y'all met while playing a crossword app?"

"BuddyWords. I like to play it on my breaks at work."

She decided to take the opening into his current life. Maybe that would be an easier route versus jumping straight into the past. "Where do you work?"

"My buddy Buck and I own a landscape company. I supervise four of our crews."

Clair's mind flooded with a memory of walking around *Blumegesellschaft*, the town's flower garden that had been founded more than a century ago by Port Provident's German immigrant garden club. "You always did enjoy being outdoors."

Rob laughed. "Cubicle life was never going to be for me."

Something about his laughter cracked the ice in the air. There were still some good memories. Maybe if she focused on those, she could make it through tonight and then move on.

"You okay?" Rob had fixed his gaze on her fingers, where they tapped a restless rhythm on the faded countertop.

"I am," she lied, using as few syllables as possible.

"Okay," he nodded. She could tell he wasn't quite sure if she was being honest with him. "You said you wanted to get together so we could talk. I guess you have some questions. Not that I blame you, I mean."

Clair took the easy way out and stared down the pasta. She kept herself busy turning off the stove and draining the thin noodles in a colander over the sink.

"I just want to know why," she said, heavily. "One day you were here and you told me you loved me and you talked about our future together. It seemed like it was so real at the time. And then, you were just gone. I never heard from you again."

FOR YEARS, ROB HAD hoped that she'd just forgotten about him.

He'd certainly never forgotten about Clair, but that had been his cross to bear. He took the memories with him when he followed his dad to South Carolina. But he'd never expected Clair to continue thinking about him for so long.

"Every time it rained, I thought about you. I thought about dancing at the lighthouse that night." Her voice sounded low and strained. She kept walking around the kitchen, kept moving.

He kept watching her.

How did he tell Clair that he never stopped loving her? That he also thought about dancing with her every time it rained? It would seem so hollow. After all, he was the one who left. Of his own free accord. And he was the one who never called or wrote. Again, he made the choice.

She'd asked for honesty. He hadn't given her anything else over the years. So, she'd asked for this one thing, and he'd give it to her. Even if it broke his heart all over again to do it.

"My dad needed me. He was leaving my mom—and that was a good thing."

Clair looked up and nodded slightly. "I remember you said he was abusive."

"He was an alcoholic. A grade-A jerk."

"So why would you go with him? Why wouldn't you stay with your mom? Didn't she need you? Her whole world was collapsing. She needed you, Rob. We all needed you here."

"She had Gretel." Now it was Rob's turn to tap his fingers. Remembering the night he'd decided to leave sent adrenaline crackling like lightning strikes through his veins. "Her world wasn't collapsing. It was starting. She was getting a new lease on life. I knew she'd be okay. But Pop...he wouldn't. He couldn't take care of himself. He'd have gotten himself killed in a year. I just knew it. I had to be a man and take care of him because he wasn't man enough to take care of himself."

Clair placed a plate and silverware in front of Rob. She stayed silent as she picked up her own dish and brought it to the table.

"So, what happened?" She sat down as she asked the question. "Why didn't you at least call or something?"

Rob closed his eyes. He could see it all so clearly. The past came back to him like a movie for one, played just behind his eyelids.

He fortified himself with a deep breath before opening his eyes again and giving Clair the honesty she'd asked for. "I was embarrassed."

"Embarrassed?" He could tell she didn't understand.

"I never went back to school. I didn't want to hear about everyone going to prom and graduation, and then on to college—knowing I'd missed it all myself. I had to go get a job. Pop couldn't hold one down and drink at the same time. We lived in the car for months before I could save up enough for an apartment."

He lowered his head and took a bite of the spaghetti.

"You didn't graduate?"

"Nope." There wasn't any way to sugar coat it. "You probably think I made a mess out of my life. I ran off to take care of my alcoholic, abusive father. I didn't go to college. I don't even have a high school diploma."

Rob had always thought he'd just done what he needed to do. But now, trying to explain it to Clair... It didn't make sense. In fact, it just sounded downright embarrassing.

He needed to change the subject. He knew he'd promised Clair he'd answer her questions. But the honesty he promised her had begun to challenge the lies he'd told himself for so long. And it had begun to make his head hurt.

"What about you? How did high school wind up for you? Who did you go to prom with?"

Maybe throwing a few questions out there would give him a moment to regroup.

"I didn't go to prom."

Clair's answer didn't buy him nearly enough time to try and get rid of the headache.

They sat there for a moment, the silence filling the room almost as thoroughly as the scent of the homemade meat sauce atop the spaghetti.

"I guess that's my fault." Rob knew he needed to own it.

Clair laid her fork down on the edge of her plate and looked straight across the small table. "No. It's mine."

"But I'm the one who left. It's okay, Clair. You can call it like it is."

"I am calling it like it is, for once. I gave you too much real estate in my heart. And then you foreclosed on it."

Hearing her assessment of the situation tore at his heart. He used a lot of tools in his line of work. Some cut, some dug, some poked. But nothing had a blade sharper than Clair's words.

"How can I make it up to you?" The words sounded hollow to him. But he didn't know what else he could offer...all he could do was try. Wasn't that the whole point of this evening? To be honest? To try?

"Tell me about your life in South Carolina. Tell me about how it was with your dad."

IT FELT STRANGE TO hear Rob tell about the years since he'd left Port Provident. She'd built it up in her mind that the reason he didn't call, didn't write, didn't have any contact rested solely on her shoulders. She'd carried that blame and guilt for so long.

If only she'd been a better girlfriend.

If only she'd been prettier.

If only she'd offered to do things with him that other high school girls did with their boyfriends—even though he'd never asked. He'd never even tried or pressured her, like so many other teenage boys did in relationships.

She'd told herself so many times that if only she'd been worth remembering, he'd have remembered.

If only…

Clair had wrapped those words of self-loathing around her like a blanket and worn them like a suit of armor, there to deflect any feeling—good or bad—from getting anywhere near her heart.

She stopped herself from grabbing hold of that blanket again and forced herself to listen to the words Rob was saying. He was doing his part. She needed to do hers.

"…and then I met Buck. I mowed lawns in the mornings with his crew and I kept the job working third shift in the warehouse. It took about two years of saving all that third shift money—it was good pay because of the shift differential—to scrape together enough to send my dad to rehab. But I did. He fought me every step of the way there. I thought we were going to come to literal blows before he got admitted. But for some reason, he stayed for the full twenty-one days. He's been sober ever since. Going on eight years."

Clair's mouth went dry. "You did what you set out to do," she said simply.

Rob nodded. "Yeah. I saved my dad. I knew he was in there somewhere. I couldn't lose him to the alcohol and the rage."

A small wiggle of warmth pushed into her chest, tearing back some of that gray cloud she'd held so close for so long. Clair stopped clearing the table. She wanted to remember how this felt. She wanted to be able to remind herself that something good came out of the events that had brought her so much sadness.

"A wise son makes his father glad," she replied, with careful consideration.

Rob's hands gestured nonchalantly. "I don't really know how happy he was with me back then."

A faint smile tugged across her lips. "It's from Proverbs in the Bible."

"Handy little book," Rob said. "Martie was quoting out of it earlier. Do y'all just sit around quoting Bible clichés at the center for the fun of it?"

Without any effort on her part, the smile on Clair's face stretched more broadly. "Only on Sundays. Jim Meadows is a retired pastor and he does a Sunday service for the residents. The rest of the time, we just quote 'em because they're the truth."

"I guess so," he shrugged.

Clair came back to the table and sat down with a fresh glass of tea. "Some days, those truths are the only things that keep me going."

"Are you doing okay, Clair? You've said a few things that make me think maybe not."

"I was diagnosed with clinical depression in college, although we suspect I had tendencies and shorter episodes for years before and then it got triggered and just didn't go away. I don't know if you know anything about depression."

He shook his head, but the warmth in his eyes gave her the strength she needed to keep talking. She could see that he truly cared about what she had to say, and as she'd learned over the years, one person truly caring could make a big difference.

"After you left, I just started to withdraw. Senior year wasn't the same. I wasn't going to prom—because who would I go with? My best friend wasn't around for me to talk to anymore. I chose to focus on my schoolwork and my grades and getting into college. But even after I went to college, I felt weighed down. The change of scenery didn't help. So, one of my professors told me about the counseling center on campus and they diagnosed me with chronic depression. They call it dysthymia. It's not as severe as some forms of depression, but it can be persistent. I have it a lot better than most people with depression, but I still have to work on myself and take care of myself."

Rob's jaw clenched. His eyes went dull and he kept them focused on some distant point on the other side of the kitchen.

"So, it's my fault?" His words cracked slightly as they came out. "Clair, I never meant to do anything that would..."

Clair took a fortifying breath and reached out a hand across the table. Softly, she laid it on the back of Rob's hand. Once upon a time, holding his hand had been second nature to her. Somehow, it didn't surprise her in the least to realize that the curves and angles still seemed familiar.

"There are things that triggered it, but it's just part of my makeup. It's how my brain works."

"Can they treat it?" He seemed almost desperate for her answer.

"I take medication. We tweak it periodically. And I have a great counselor who helps me when I need a little extra support. Thankfully, I haven't needed to call her in a while. But I also try and control it with exercise and good nutrition and things like that. One day, I really hope I can be done with the meds. I truly believe I can. I work toward that every single day. The hope of it keeps me going."

She removed her hand from Rob's, noticing the small lingering feel of heat on the palm of her hand. Standing up, Clair began to remove the rest of the dishes from the table to the sink a few steps away.

"But what can I do to help? What can I do for you?"

She'd asked him for honesty. She'd learned that he'd left because he'd had a loyalty to his father and had to go quickly to keep up with his father's hasty, unplanned actions. She'd heard him speak about working multiple jobs at all hours of the day to save enough money to send his dad to a program to get a fresh start.

He'd carried as much of a burden as she had during the years since they'd last seen each other.

In fact, if Clair was being fully honest—Rob had carried a greater burden. He'd carried the load for not just himself and his own food and shelter and such, but that of his father. And that father hadn't acted in a way to deserve a son who dropped all the potential of his own future in order to save another man from the demons of his past.

Now, Rob had returned to make amends with those he'd left behind.

And as soon as his path crossed with Clair's, he prioritized righting that relationship as well.

Clair realized she didn't just owe Rob Landers honesty.

She owed him a second chance.

"Could we be friends?" As soon as the words came out of her mouth, she regretted saying them. It sounded so silly. So high school.

Maybe that was fitting, after all. Maybe nothing really had changed.

Rob brought the bread basket over and placed it on the counter near where Clair stood.

He closed the distance between them with one solid step, then reached out an arm. His hand fit loosely over the curve of her hip, just like it had a hundred times before—and a thousand times in her dreams.

She challenged herself to look in his eyes. Like the feel of his hand, they hadn't changed either. The dark gray rings in the center still had the look of winter and smoke.

"Clair, I've been gone a long time. And there have been a lot of miles between us. But never has there been one second of one day that's passed where I have not considered you a friend."

He pulled her close and wrapped his arms around her waist. The armor around her heart had been in place for so long, but she knew this feeling. He would be gone again soon. It would be okay to allow herself to feel the warmth as his arms pressed against the small of her back. It would be okay to remind herself of what had once been good.

She'd wanted to forget so much since Rob had been gone.

But a hug seemed okay to remember.

Clair had asked Rob here tonight so that she could move forward. And now that he was here, and the air had cleared, it surprised her to realize that she'd moved forward into his arms. And that it felt like no time had passed at all.

Chapter Four

THE RETIREMENT CENTER'S multi-purpose room had begun to fill with crepe-paper streamers, ribbons, colorful hearts, fuchsia tablecloths, white bunting, and flowers. Lots and lots of flowers.

So many flowers.

For the first time in years, the sight of decorations piled up for the May Day dance didn't tug at her own heart with regret about the one dance she'd missed out on a decade ago.

Three days ago, she and Rob hadn't just shared dinner. They'd shared the stories of the years. They'd shared honesty. And they shared the foundations of a bridge between them.

Depression's roots didn't grow in shallow soil. They grew in the areas of the brain where the most elemental chemicals of personality and mood lived—or in the case of patients like her, *didn't* live. The world had been muted for long enough that Clair knew no single conversation would flip a switch and magically cure her.

Depression didn't work like that. Life wasn't a fairy tale.

But yet, for the first time in so long, she didn't feel quite so weighed down. The blanket she'd clutched so tightly all these years seemed to slip just a little bit. She could feel a speck of sun settling on her shoulders.

It felt warm. It felt clear. It felt good.

And she was determined to not just enjoy the feeling, but to build upon it. Rob revealed he'd be in Port Provident for a few weeks. A few weeks more of honesty and coming to terms with what had happened in their past could definitely jumpstart her healing. Clair even allowed to dare herself to hope that settling this in her mind really could be the first step to tapering down her medication—or perhaps even weaning off entirely.

It might be the key to the dream that, even in her darkest hours, she'd never given up on.

As she unpacked another box of balloons to blow up later, Clair thought about a verse from the Old Testament that her grandmother used to tell her, when Clair would face trials growing up. "But as for you, be strong and do not give up, for your work will be rewarded."

She would never quit working toward her ultimate goal.

"And Lord, I believe in Your promises. I believe that I will be rewarded with seeing this goal come to pass." Clair said the words softly to herself, but she knew the right ears would hear.

"Do you need some help?" The voice echoed in the room.

Clair's shoulders shot up and she rose onto the balls of her feet. Quickly, she turned her head around. It was Rob.

His hands were wrapped around a bouquet of yellow roses. Each golden bloom was fully open, and the way the greenery and small white baby's breath mingled around the stems took Clair's breath away.

"You brought sunshine," she said with a smile, enjoying the view—of both Rob's smile and the flowers.

He stopped a few steps short of Clair and held out the arrangement. "They're for you."

Clair stood up and laid the packages of pink-and-red balloons on the nearest table. "For me?"

Rob's smile didn't fade. "I saw them in the store a little while ago, and they reminded me of dinner the other night."

"These remind you of spaghetti?" Clair reached out for the bouquet he offered. She leaned her head close and took in a deep breath. They smelled heavenly. Rich and sweet, the scent was the perfect compliment to her earlier thoughts.

"Not quite," Rob said with a laugh. "I told you that there was never a time while I was gone that I didn't still consider you a friend. I want you to believe it. They say yellow roses are the official flower of friendship."

Clair kept her nose buried in the yellow center of the centermost flower. "They do?"

A flash crackled through her mind. She wished they were red roses.

Instead of mere friendship, she wished there hadn't been a day when he wasn't still in love with her.

Because there hadn't been a day when Clair hadn't been in love with Rob. Even through all the what-ifs and the second-guessing, Rob was still her first love. In truth, he was still her only love.

"My sister used to say that. Of course, the yellow rose is the official flower of Texas, too. So, if you'd rather ascribe something Texan to them, that's okay too. They're just flowers."

Clair looked up and his eyes drew her in. "No, no I don't want to make them just Texan. They're lovely, and the sentiment behind them is lovely, too."

"I'm glad you like them." Rob pointed at the pile of boxes in the corner. "It looks like you've got a bit of a mess going on here. Do you need some help?"

"Those are the decorations for the centerpieces on the table. And then that stack in the middle is for the DJ booth. It usually takes me about two days to get all the decorations out and in the right places."

Rob headed straight for the pile and started digging through a box. "Well, if you have two more hands, then it should cut the time in half, right?"

Clair raised an eyebrow. She couldn't argue with the logic—or afford to turn down the help. "No one ever accused me of being a math whiz, but that's some division I can get behind."

By the time Clair's stomach let out a loud grumble, several hours had passed by.

"Was that you?" Rob's voice held more than a hint of teasing.

It seemed pointless to deny it, considering they were the only two in the activity hall. "It's like an alarm."

"Time for lunch," he replied, then looked down at his watch. "Whoa. Actually, time for dinner. Do you think we're at a stopping point?"

Clair leaned back slightly on her heels and rubbed her lower back. "This is where I'd hoped to be by lunch time tomorrow. It looks amazing in here."

Rob began to pack rolls of tape back in a cardboard box on the central table. "It looks like prom."

Even the mere thought of prom made Clair pause. It always had. And now, here she was, standing in the same room with the person who should have been her date to that teenage rite-of-passage.

"It does," she acknowledged.

"Do you have a date...here...to retirement prom?" Rob gestured at the decorations. Judging by the pauses in his sentence, Clair wondered if the memories were creeping up on him, too.

She shook her head. "Nope. This is a work event."

And thank goodness for that, she thought. Keeping her head focused on the business aspect made it possible for her to put this event on every year for her residents. They loved it. She had to keep up the tradition for them. They didn't need to make a sacrifice for her disappointing memories.

"I understand," Rob said. He tucked the last of the supplies in the box. "Would you come to dinner with me?"

Clair did a double-take, remembering the first time he'd asked her out. She forced a deep breath into her lungs before answering. She needed to leave the past in the past and make decisions based on the present. And in the present, Rob was a guy who had given her honesty, cleared the air, brought her friendship-colored flowers, and created a whimsical May pole as the centerpiece of this annual dance. If she judged him on his current actions, then she could say yes with some degree of confidence, knowing she'd actually enjoyed the small talk today and the time in his presence.

"Sure. Where?"

"I'd love a pizza at Seahorse."

Pizza. Casual. Cheese. Crust. Perfect. See? She could do this. She could be a normal person instead of a shell going through the motions. One step closer to her goal.

"I'll meet you there in an hour."

ROB HAD SUGGESTED THE Seahorse, Port Provident's best-known casual eatery, not just because he'd never had a slice of pizza that compared since he left town. More than even that, he picked it because there were only good memories here. Hanging out with friends after school. Pouring blue cheese dressing over Buffalo wings. Dropping quarters in the jukebox at the back to play favorite songs from Top 40 radio.

He loved everything about this place.

And he loved Clair's smile.

By bringing her back to a place she'd loved as a teenager, he hoped to bring some of that happiness back to her now. He didn't want her to fear the memories. They'd made lots of good ones.

And hopefully, now that he was here in Port Provident for a few weeks—and they were setting things right between them—they could make a few more.

After dinner, Rob felt peace in his heart. They'd shared a pizza, but more than that, they shared laughs and memories—just as he'd hoped. As they stood on the sidewalk at the edge of the parking lot, Rob knew he didn't want the evening to end.

Maybe he didn't deserve much more.

But he wanted more.

Looking at Clair's dark blond hair with streaks of honey and brown sugar, and seeing the way her smile settled casually on her lips made him remember everything he'd once said. All those dreams and teenaged certainties—they all came flooding back every time he looked at Clair. He couldn't erase the past, but he could close the gap.

"Is it still out there?"

"Is what still out there?"

Rob put his hands in his pockets. "The lighthouse. Is it still at the end of the island?"

Clair's eyes went wide as she figured out his question. "Of course. It's been here a lot longer than any of us have, and I have no doubt it will still be there long after we're gone."

"Want to come with me? I'd like to see it again."

His heart paused. His lungs filled and held. Everything in him waited for Clair's *yes* or *no*.

"But it's getting dark."

"Clair. It's a lighthouse. There's light."

He knew she didn't realize it, but there was light in her too. Maybe he could make her see that once more. He just needed more time with her.

She made a funny face, wrinkling her nose slightly. "Duh. Sure. I guess I can go. Your car or mine?"

"I'll drive. I haven't driven that stretch of road in a long time. I miss it."

"It hasn't changed," Clair said quietly. "Not much has. Port Provident seems to stay the same."

Rob opened the door to his sister's compact sedan for Clair. "I think that's one of the things I love the most about it. When I was younger, I thought this place was kind of boring. I guess I thought going out to save my dad would be a bit of an adventure. I built it up in my mind. I could save him and see a little bit of the world beyond this sandbar. But now, seeing it all again, it's the same as it ever was. And it feels like home."

After they got in the car and began to drive to the western tip of Provident Island, Clair cleared her throat. Rob tuned his attention to her.

"You said Port Provident still feels like home. Do you ever think you'll stay? Or are you going back to the east coast?"

The sound of an old power ballad floated out of the car's speakers.

"It's been really good spending some time with my mom and my sister." Rob pulled off the main road and into the parking lot at the Port Provident lighthouse. "I don't know. I think I'd like to stay. But it depends on if they want me here longer—I don't want to be a burden on their hospitality or anything like that. I can always come back later, now that we're resetting those lines of communication. And also, my dad's been sober for a long time, but I need to be certain he won't need my support."

"That sounds reasonable," Clair said as she unbuckled her seatbelt and got out of the car. She walked to the edge of the grass. The sound of the waves slapping the rocks below rode above the low howl of the breeze at Point Provident.

Rob stopped just behind Clair as she turned to face him.

"What about me?" Her words felt heavy as they were spoken into the air around them. "Do I play into your plans at all? Now that we've reset our own lines of communication, I mean."

He wanted to tell her *of course*. He wanted to put his arms around her and pull her tight against the evening chill. He wanted to kiss her and let emotion say the things he didn't quite feel like he could verbalize right now.

But he didn't want to scare her off.

Those lines she just acknowledged meant too much to him.

Did he let himself hope that they were beginning to mean something to her too?

"Do you want me to stay a little longer?"

He wanted to know her answer. But he also knew that by wanting it so badly, she still held his heart in her hands. The years, the distance, the misunderstandings didn't matter.

All that mattered was her.

She nodded. The wind whipped up and tossed the ends of her hair around her shoulders.

"I'd like it." She tucked her restless hair behind her ears. "It's starting to rain."

Rob looked up at the fine mist falling from the sky. Here and there, a larger drop mixed in. Then they increased in frequency.

"I think that's our cue," he said, holding out his hand.

Clair's eyebrows pulled together, creating a furrow in her forehead. "What do you mean?"

"Dancing in the rain. It's what we do. Isn't it, Clair?"

The lines between her eyes smoothed as a smile slipped across her face. She placed her hand in his, and Rob pulled her close.

He thought he'd come back to Port Provident to set things right.

But he knew now he'd come back for this. To capture what had been. And to bring it back to life.

They swayed together for a moment, then he leaned his head down toward hers. Everything about this moment had a sense of contentment.

"I shouldn't have brought you yellow roses, Clair."

She pulled back and looked him in the eye. Rob could see a trace of hurt fog across her gaze.

"I should have brought you red ones. I told you there was never a moment when I didn't think of you as a friend. But that's not true, and I promised you honesty. There's never been a moment when you weren't the love of my life."

She opened her mouth slightly, as though she were about to speak.

Rob leaned down and pressed his lips to hers, cutting off anything but the truth he'd carried with him for all these years.

He'd always loved her.

And when she kissed him back, Rob knew Clair's own truth. She'd always loved him, too.

Chapter Five

"I'M SAVING THAT SEAT," Martie said, patting the white folding chair to her right.

Clair eyed her with curiosity. "For whom?"

For the last two years, Clair had always sat next to Martie at the Sunday morning service in the small chapel at the retirement community.

"For Rob," Martie said in a tone that didn't leave Clair much room to ask the questions that immediately popped into her head.

As far as Clair knew, Rob hadn't ever set foot in a church. He certainly didn't when she knew him in Port Provident. Maybe after his dad got sober, they started attending in South Carolina.

"You know me. I like to invite all my friends to Sunday service and lunch. It reminds me of having my girls around. I love family and friends and Sunday. They just all seem to go together."

"I can't argue with you there, Martie. Can I sit over here?"

"Nope. Linda's got those saved. You can sit on the other side of Rob."

It shouldn't have sent a little click of electricity through her system. She'd seen Rob several times since the night when they danced—and then shared a sweet, hopeful kiss—in the rain under the shadow of the lighthouse. In fact, they'd seen each other daily—sometimes for just a few minutes, sometimes for a meal. Last night, he'd stopped by the apartment for another round of pasta. This time, they paired it with a movie on TV.

Life seemed to be easing right back into the routine they'd had years ago.

Only church had never been something they shared.

"Am I late?" Rob loudly whispered toward Martie from the main aisle.

"Nope. Come on down!" She patted the empty seat.

Rob worked his way around the feet and knees of the others who were already seated. When he took his spot, Clair could smell the deep spruce notes of his cologne. He hadn't changed the brand since he'd started wearing it. Living on a beach didn't lend itself to many things that reminded her of the vacations her family used to take to the Colorado mountains. But Rob's cologne always did. It smelled fresh. It smelled cozy. It triggered thoughts of comfort in her mind.

Suddenly, Clair smiled. It had happened. Thoughts of Rob no longer set off nervousness or regret to stream through her body. In such a short time, so many years and misunderstandings had been cleared.

The breakthrough she'd prayed about having for so long had come.

"Thank you," she said softly. She knew God would know exactly what she meant. She knew it was only because of Him that she could experience this new beginning and this new path forward.

"Um? You're welcome?" Rob's quick look showed confusion.

A laugh made Clair's head shake slightly. "Not you."

"So, you're thanking yourself?"

"Not exactly that, either."

"I don't get it," Rob said. "Am I supposed to?"

Clair remembered their promise of honesty. She also remembered her teenage hopes that Rob would come to church with her and that a shared faith would be part of their happily-ever-after, something they could build upon for the family they talked of creating together.

And now, here he was. Yes, Martie had invited Rob. But Clair had never believed in coincidence. Rob was here, next to her, because it was the next step on the road to healing their hearts.

"One day you will," she said, believing it with certainty and hope.

The choir filed into their seats at the front of the room and the organist began to play the introduction to one of Clair's favorite hymns. Rob settled in the chair, then raised his arm and lowered it behind Clair's back. His palm gently cupped her shoulder.

They turned to each other at the same time and smiled.

"Be strong and do not give up..." the verse she'd clung to for years came back to mind. This security was the reward she'd been praying for. She'd always thought that she'd find her way out of the darkness when she had all the answers.

She didn't know she'd find it when she was back in Rob's arms.

ROB PACED UP AND DOWN the long hallway, his cellphone glued to his ear. He couldn't believe what he was hearing.

"So, you saw him at the bar last night, man?"

Jape Jones was one of Rob's father's closest friends. They worked together at the garage. On the weekends, they rode motorcycles together around the backroads of South Carolina.

"Yeah, Rob. I was picking my nephew up from his job at the sports bar down the street and I saw your dad walking in. He had his arm around someone. They looked like they were holding each other up. I tried calling him, but the phone kept going to voicemail. I wouldn't have called you, but I feel like something is going on. This ain't like him."

Now there, Jape was wrong. This was like Rick Landers. The old Rick Landers. The Rick Landers who didn't think twice about downing a bottle of whatever he could get his hands on first, then berating his wife and his kids at the top of his lungs.

But that Rick Landers hadn't been seen for close to eight years. Not since Rob wrestled him into rehab.

But Rob had been gone for almost two weeks.

He ended the call, then kicked at the baseboard along the floor. He should have known better. You can't ever fully trust an alcoholic.

Or an alcoholic's son.

What would Clair say when he told her he had to leave—again?

The thought left him ice cold. How could he possibly make her understand that he loved her, but he had to go?

He couldn't. He knew it. It would be asking too much of her heart to put her through walking away again. If he left this time, it would have to be the last time.

And he *had* to leave.

His father's life depended upon it. Rob needed to get there and get his dad help. He would not let Rick completely fall off the wagon. He couldn't.

Rob ran a hand through his hair and cursed the fact that he'd let himself think about staying longer in Port Provident—about maybe even moving back here. Since reconnecting with Clair, he'd found a part of his soul that had been dormant inside. It was the best part of him, the part of him that had never stopped loving the first girl he ever kissed and belonged here on the Texas coast with her.

"You know, wheelchairs can leave scuff marks along the wall if you hit it just the right way. But I think that's nothing compared to the dent you just left." Martie's eyes narrowed to a squint and she placed one hand solidly on her hip. "Care to tell me what's going on, Rob?"

Rob clenched his jaw. He didn't want to tell Martie anything. Mostly, he didn't want to admit his whole world had just collapsed. Again.

"Not really."

"You kicked a defenseless wall. Something's gotten to you."

He'd seen dogs guard bones less fiercely than how Martie was currently reacting. It was a narrow hallway. There was no way he was getting around her without coming clean, at least a little bit.

"I have to go."

"But we haven't had Sunday lunch yet. It's the second Sunday of the month. Ham."

"I can't. Thanks for inviting me, though."

The steel in her gaze pinned him to the wall. "Have you told Clair?"

"Not yet. I just got the call. But I've got to get a flight back home and go. It's my dad."

Martie nodded knowingly. "Is he going to be okay?"

Rob shrugged. "Martie, I honestly don't know. It's all a big mess."

"I'm a mom, a grandma. I understand. Family comes first. We'll miss you at the dance tonight."

The dance. It was May first. May Day. Yet another thing he'd ruin for Clair...it was *déjà vu* all over again, or however the saying went. Air pushed through his teeth and came out with a hissing sound.

"Do you know where Clair is?" He'd lost track of her after the church service ended. She'd stayed behind talking with some family members of a new resident.

"She had to head to the mainland. Something about having to pick up the big shiny balloons and the corsages."

Rob reached out and took Martie's hand and squeezed. "Will you tell her I had to go?"

Martie didn't say a word. She bobbed her head briefly.

Rob thought he saw the gleam of a tear in the older woman's eye.

"Also, tell her I know she won't want to talk to me again—and I understand—but I'll think of dancing with her every time it rains."

THERE WERE FLOWERS and hearts and streamers everywhere.

The red roses in the centerpieces mocked her.

I shouldn't have brought you yellow roses, Clair... I should have brought you red ones.

She heard Rob's declaration from the lighthouse every time a crimson bloom caught her eye. And since there were approximately one-thousand-two-hundred-and-seventy-one of them in the frivolously-decorated multi-purpose room...well, those words rung in her ears like a doorbell being attacked by a toddler.

May Day now felt even more hollow than the night of senior prom. At least back then, she had the time to make excuses and plan something else to do with her time. But hosting this prom for senior citizens was her job. She had to be here. She had to smile and watch couples sway to the sounds of big band music and ballads.

There was no choice but to stand in a room of people she cared for deeply and ignore the fact that her heart was breaking a little more with every minute that passed.

"He didn't want to go, dear." Martie placed a soft hand on Clair's shoulder and patted.

Clair knew Martie meant the gesture as comfort. But it didn't matter. And whether or not Rob wanted to go didn't matter, either.

He was gone and the gray clouds were back.

She had been so stupid for ever thinking they could go away. It was just how her brain worked. Clair needed to accept that and the fact that she'd always need medication and mild, but constant, depression would be her status quo.

Just like Rob had left for his status quo, back to South Carolina.

"It doesn't really matter, Martie. He's gone. We don't need to talk about it."

"But maybe we do, my dear. I know how it feels to get left behind, remember? I miss my girls so much."

Clair punched a button on the light machine. "But they had to go. They had jobs."

"So did Rob. He had an obligation to his father. His father needed him."

But I needed him, too. Clair didn't want to say it out loud, but she heard the words as clearly as though she'd spoken them.

"Clair, I think he's an honorable man."

Before Rob returned to town, Clair wouldn't have agreed. But now, knowing what she knew about why he'd left in the first place—knowing how he'd scraped together the money to get his father the treatment he needed—Clair couldn't disagree with Martie's assessment.

"He is," she replied.

"You know what I told Rob before he had dinner with you that first time?"

Clair felt her brow wrinkle. "No. I didn't know y'all really talked."

"He's my friend. And so are you. And I think what I told him applies to you too. Proverbs 28:25 says 'selfishness only causes trouble—you are much better off to trust the Lord.' His father needs him. He came back once. You need to trust that he'll come back again."

"Are you saying I'm being selfish?" Clair wanted to argue fiercely against the very idea.

Martie patted Clair's shoulder again, absently. "Not in so many words, my dear. But I think he feels like he has to choose one or the other of you. I think you would both be happier if you found a way to let him know you'll still be here."

Clair's mouth went dry. She didn't know how to answer Martie.

"The DJ's taking requests. I'm going to go leave him some suggestions." She lifted her hand. "Think about what I said, though, okay?"

"Okay," Clair said. She would have more than enough time with her thoughts tonight.

About ten o'clock, the DJ played the last song. Balloons dropped from a net strung up on the ceiling. The last of the partygoers cheered as the pink and white and red ovals fell to the dance floor and bounced around.

And then, just like that, it was over.

The residents went back to their rooms and apartments, presumably headed for a good night's sleep and dreams of swirling and twirling steps.

Clair should have started cleaning up—otherwise, tomorrow would be a long day. Instead, she sat heavily in a chair near the center table.

"Did I miss it all?"

Clair turned around and saw Rob just inside the doorway.

"It ended about half an hour ago. I thought you were headed home."

He crossed the room in a few strides. "I thought so too."

"Martie said your dad was sick."

Rob pulled up one of the white chairs and straddled it as he sat down. "Not sick. Relapsed. His buddy called me and said he saw Dad walking into a bar. I couldn't let him ruin everything he'd worked for. I had to get to him before he self-destructed again."

Clair studied the lines and angles of his face. His jaw was set with determination.

"So why are you here?"

He took his phone from his pocket and placed it on the table. "Dad finally answered my call as I was about to board a plane in Houston."

"Where was he?"

"At an AA meeting with his sponsor, Larry. Larry relapsed, not my dad. My dad was getting Larry a cab when Jape drove by and saw them. Jape misread what he saw. After getting the cab, my dad got Larry to a meeting. He hasn't left Larry's side for forty-eight hours and they're checking him into a clinic in the morning." He tapped the table nervously and let out a deep breath. "My dad's going to be okay. He stayed strong. He saved his buddy."

Clair's heart softened with every word Rob spoke. "It seems to me he had a good example several years ago when he needed someone to be strong for him."

"I didn't want to leave you, Clair—now or then—but he's my dad. I remember who he was before the bottle got him and destroyed our family. All I've ever wanted was for my dad to be the man he was before he started drinking. I got this crazy idea in my head that I could save him."

"And you did." Clair reached for Rob's hand.

"But I lost you in the process."

She slid one hand on either side of his and squeezed. "I never left. I've always been here, just waiting for the sun to shine again."

Slowly, Rob stood. Clair raised herself as well, still holding his hand.

He pulled her close. "Dance with me. In the sunshine. In the rain. I don't care, as long as I'm holding you. Whatever season life brings, I want to know we're going through it together."

Clair lifted to the tips of her toes and turned her face toward Rob. She saw hope in his eyes and knew it was mirrored in her own.

"Be strong and do not give up," she whispered the heart of her favorite verse as her lips came within a hair's breadth of Rob's.

"Never. I never have." He inched his face closer and smoothed back her hair with his free hand.

Clair breathed in the fresh spruce of his cologne. In all the years they'd been apart, it hadn't changed. And neither had Rob. He'd go to the ends of the earth to stand by the people he loved.

She knew now, beyond all doubt, that he still loved her too.

She could be strong in that love, knowing that it would stand by her in the years to come.

Clair closed her eyes and murmured as she touched her lips, feather light, to Rob's.

"And I never will. May I have this dance? Forever."

You Don't Have to Leave Port Provident!

Start First Kiss Fireworks Now!

DR. AMANDA MCGOVERN was headed to Europe for a research-filled summer sabbatical that would secure her promotion to a tenured professor...until a funding shortage at Provident College closes her project. As the semester comes to an end, the college is abuzz with rumors about the after-effects of a serious concussion jeopardizing the slowly-healing relationship between Provident College head baseball coach Dane Vazquez and his estranged son. Amanda doesn't trust her heart, but she does trust her knowledge of the human brain. It may not be the international research sabbatical she has been counting on—but there may be summer fireworks. Will they be enough to ignite her career...and her heart?

If you love quick, sweet escape romance stories filled with hope, heart, and happily-ever-after that will make you swoon and leave you with a smile, you will want to celebrate the holidays with the residents of the beachside small town of Port Provident.

https://books2read.com/FirstKissFireworksBook

Join Kristen's Reader Community Today and Receive a Free Port Provident Story

Join Kristen's reader community today for the latest and get A Place to Find Love, *a sweet escape romance that introduces you to Port Provident, Texas and the residents who find love on the island, for free!*
www.kristenethridge.com/newsletter[1]

---

1. http://www.kristenethridge.com/newsletter

Sneak Peek: First Kiss Fireworks—Chapter One

"SO I HEARD YOU'RE STARTING your summer vacation a little bit early this year."

Amanda McGovern looked up from her desk. She could feel the frown lines etched into her face. Her week had started with back-to-back long, frustrating days.

"A little early? It looks like I'm starting a whole semester early," she said.

Roger Caldwell, the chair of the Education Department at Provident College, leaned against the door jamb of Amanda's office. "Looks like it. So, did they give you any indication at all? Or did they just tell you that the funding was canceled?"

"Well, I mean what else are they really going to say, Roger? I got the feeling from Stavros that the whole thing was kind of embarrassing."

Roger laughed little under his breath. "I'll say. The whole thing's more than just kind of embarrassing. It's totally embarrassing. I mean, having to completely shut the doors to the Institute?"

"Well, they're not completely shutting the doors," Amanda's thoughts on the subject which now defined her life rolled out on an exasperated sigh. "I think they're still going to have basic classes. But all the peripheral programs are getting the ax. It stinks because I really feel like this program was on the cutting edge. We were finally going to be able to do the research that might lead to providing an option to kids who are struggling to focus in the classroom, due to ADHD or autism, and other similar, brain-related disorders. Right now, it so difficult for them to concentrate and the only thing most professionals have to offer are high-powered pharmaceuticals. What if there's a better answer? I believe there is. I've been waiting to be part of this research for almost two years—it's been my passion, my mission. And now because some politicians can't balance their budgets, the funding is revoked and the whole program is shut down. Instead of diving in with one of the world's leading experts in my field for a short summer research sabbatical, now I have to exchange a plane ticket to Europe and figure out where my work and I go from here."

"I know you're disappointed," her boss said. "And I hate to come here and be the bearer of even more bad news, but we have got to figure out what to do with you for this semester."

"What to do with me?" Amanda said. Her eyebrows pushed upward into the furrows that had crisscrossed her forehead since she hung up the phone call with Stavros yesterday afternoon. "What do you mean—*what to do with me*?"

Roger adjusted his glasses on the bridge of his nose. Amanda had studied with Roger as an undergrad, and now had worked with him for several years. She knew the little signs and gestures he began to make when he was uncomfortable with the message he was delivering.

"I mean, the Institute, Amanda. Well, specifically, I mean their program money—that's what was paying you this semester while you were researching with them. Your salary was being reimbursed through this program. No program, no research funds. No research funds, no full salary. And as far as things here at Provident College, you're not on the teaching schedule for the summer semester and it starts in less than a week. If we have to add another section to some class, I'll call you first, but I can't make any guarantees on that."

Amanda stared blankly past Roger, shaking her head slightly. She could feel the motion, powered by disbelief. The back-and-forth twist seemed futile, like laundry dangling in the breeze.

That's exactly what she was now, a college professor dangling in the breeze because of currency instabilities halfway around the world.

"Okay," she said hesitantly, trying to sort her way toward something positive. "You need me here for something, right, Roger?"

"Well," her boss said wryly. "Not for teaching classes. Are you still going to be able to do any of your research?"

"I don't think so," Amanda said. The weight of realization started to stack brick-by-brick on her shoulders, pushing them down. She felt the heaviness so strongly that it caused the breath in her chest to squeeze tightly. "When I talked to Stavros, it sounded like the whole thing is shut down, permanently. He's no longer researching the protocol, therefore I can't assist him. What am I going to do, Roger? I can't just take some kind of unpaid sabbatical. It's not like I've got unlimited funds in my bank so I can go down to Gulfview Boulevard and play on the beach for a few months of extended time off with nothing to do."

Amanda swallowed, tasting a bitter tang of worry. Her mouth filled with something like the sharp alkaline flavor of magnesium powder. She hated coming across as desperate to someone who'd mentored her for almost her entire academic career, but she couldn't get away from the reality of no real paycheck, so to speak, coming in for a few months.

And it wasn't just being able to pay the bills. Not being able to do this research could very well push her off the tenure-track she'd worked so hard to get on.

"Let me talk to Marty. We'll see what we can do," Roger said, referencing the Dean of the College of Arts and Sciences. "We're low on options and time, so don't get your hopes up—but maybe there's something I haven't thought of."

Another harsh breath forced past Amanda's lips before she spoke. "Don't worry, Roger. I'm not sure my hopes could get any lower at this point. You know how when you're wading out at the beach and then all of a sudden, you step off the sandbar and everything's deeper? In the last twenty-four hours, I've lost track of how many sandbars I've stepped off of. I'm just treading water right now."

Roger wrapped up the conversation with a few well-meaning platitudes, but Amanda didn't hear a single one. Her eyes darted around her office, looking at the textbooks and diplomas and mementos that had so far made up her career as an educator teaching the next generation of educators how to make a difference for students with challenges. Slowly, her gaze came to rest on a photo of Amanda and her mother in front of a church in Mexico they'd attended a mission trip for a few summers ago.

The simplicity of the cinderblock building, painted a gentle shade of pale yellow brought back memories of hard work and pushing past boundaries.

Slowly, she took a deep breath and tried to shake off the feeling of drowning.

Amanda locked her eyes on the vision of the little church, wishing she could be there again, surrounded by community and a supportive group focused on achieving goals and supporting others.

But nothing kept away the feelings of being battered by the turn of the tide in her life.

She lowered her head into her hands and pressed her fingertips in the space between her eyebrows, trying to relieve the pressure inside.

"I need a life preserver. God, is there one out there?"

"DR. MCGOVERN?" DANE Vasquez felt like he was meeting someone on a blind date. Only this time, he felt a complete lack of confidence—and that almost never happened when he took someone out. He believed in only a handful of things in this life. His ability to turn a double play when the game was on the line was one. His ability to get a woman to say yes to a second date was another.

There wouldn't be any appetizers or cocktails right now in the faculty and staff dining hall at Provident College. Only Dane, a professor he'd never met, and a hope against all hope that this woman had the answers he needed.

"Yes, I'm Amanda McGovern. I'm sorry, I don't believe we've met."

"No, I don't think we have. I haven't been here at Provident College very long." Dane wanted to stick his hand out in the time-honored gesture of greeting, but there was no denying his palms were slick with more than a little trepidation. "I'm the head coach for the Provident College Tidal Waves baseball team."

"Oh, baseball. That explains it. I'm usually on this side of campus. How can I help you, coach?"

Dane gestured to the seat across the table from her. "Is it okay if I sit for just a minute?"

She pointed at the empty space. "Sure. I was just grabbing a quick bite by myself today."

"I'm sure you're busy with trying to get your last-minute details in order with the semester about to start. I eat quick lunches in crazy places while the season's going on." The color of her eyes changed from topaz to a dark golden velvet. Briefly, his mind wondered what the change indicated. But, he didn't have time to indulge that rabbit trail. He needed to ask her his question. "I need some help, and I think you might have the right background for it."

"Well, if it's baseball-related, you're probably looking for my brother." Her mouth twisted up a little at the corner, revealing a shallow dimple. "But you said this *wasn't* about baseball, Coach. So how can I help?" She lifted the glass of iced tea in front of her and took a sip.

"I understand you're a specialist in the area of students and brains and focus and concentration and things like that."

She placed the glass back on the white coaster. "Something like that. My CV has some fancier language, but yes, that's basically my area of focus. I teach the next generation of educators how to best work with children who have barriers to focus and behavior, like ADHD or autism or other conditions. I assume the individual members of your team are connected with the resources available to them at the Academic and Athletic Success Center, if they need some help, right?"

"Yeah, the guys do all their study hall hours and those who are eligible for tutoring get it. My request isn't for the whole team. It's for one guy."

Dane had been in a lot of big moments, big games. He'd had a lot of eyes watching him. He'd made the final out and preserved a win for his team more times than he could count. He wasn't used to being nervous. As long as his cleats were on, Dane usually felt like there wasn't anything he couldn't do.

But today he was here, in the dining hall, in front of Professor McGovern. He didn't have his cleats or any of his other good-luck charms to appease any of the superstitions baseball players were known for having.

All he had was his heart. And it was beating so erratically he thought that he might pass out. But Cole needed him. He couldn't give up.

This wasn't a game, but he had to save the situation anyway. For Cole. For all the times Dane hadn't been there.

"What do you mean? Usually all requests go through the Success Center. I'm pretty limited as to what I can do with regard to academic tutoring and such. It's not really my thing."

Dane decided to lay it all out on the table. Either she'd understand, or she'd reject the request. Cole's options were sliding away, like watching sand drop through the neck of an hour glass. It made Dane feel helpless. And that meant he had to settle down his beating heart and ask for what he needed.

He wasn't even against begging, but the woman in front of him with the low ponytail and striped knit blouse seemed way too classy to fall for that trick.

"He doesn't need tutoring. He's tried that. Cole was hit by a pitch last year. It hit him just above the temple. He hasn't passed any of his concussion protocols since then, but I'm not asking for your help to try and get him back on the field. He's just barely keeping up with his classes, but it's not because of the material—he doesn't need tutoring. He said his brain is constantly in a fog and he can't focus on doing his work. He sits down to read or to write a paper and after ten minutes, he is done. He's on to something else. He can't concentrate. The doctors said all they can tell him to do is rest. But if he can't get focused and get his grades up, I'm going to have to take him off scholarship."

"What year is he?" She seemed to be considering his plea.

"He's a freshman. This is his first year at Provident College."

A student worker placed a plate in front of Dr. McGovern. She smiled and told her thank you and said she'd hoped the young woman had spent a good summer at home. The student smiled and said she had, and she was looking forward to starting her student teaching in the fall. It seemed like they knew each other well, and Dane couldn't help but notice the sound of respect in the student's voice.

He needed someone who was sharp, who was respected, on his team for this project. He just needed Amanda McGovern to agree to at least meet Cole. Dane had done his research. There wasn't anyone else on Provident Island who had the skills or the background to give Cole any new hope.

"That's really awesome that you started his scholarship anyway after he was injured before enrolling." She smiled warmly.

"Well, I needed to. I'm his dad."

"Oh, so you're pulling double-duty, Coach Dad."

The phrase got under his skin a bit. He'd never coached Cole in a single game. Dane was both Cole's coach and his dad strictly in name only. "I guess you could say that."

"Well, I'm sure you've been told there's no magic bullet to help someone recover from a Traumatic Brain Injury. TBIs are unique. Everyone tends to respond in their own way. And you're right, most neurologists recommend rest because that's the generally-accepted protocol."

Dane felt his thumping heart fall to his feet. This pursuit had been for nothing.

"So you're saying there are no other options?"

The professor shook her head.

"I'm not saying that at all. There aren't many conventional options. But the brain is a complex organ, and most people who work with it will admit that they only know the tip of the iceberg about what it does and how it works. I certainly feel that way with the research and teaching I do." She tapped her finger on the table resolutely. "In fact, speaking of research, come to my office in Porter Hall in the morning. Bring Cole. Will ten o'clock work for you?"

"We can make it work."

All Cole needed was a chance. Dane would make anything work to prove to his son that this time, his dad was in it for the long haul.

Keep reading First Kiss Fireworks
Click here: https://books2read.com/FirstKissFireworksBook

The Holiday Hearts Series

The Right Resolution[1]
The Cupid Caper[2]
Lucky in Love[3]
May I Have This Dance[4]
First Kiss Fireworks[5]
Falling Forever This Time[6]
Thankful for Love[7]
Mission: Mistletoe[8]

Want to extend your stay in Port Provident?
Start reading the Hearts and Hope Series

Shelter from the Storm[9]
The Doctor's Unexpected Family[10]
His Texas Princess[11]

1. http://www.books2read.com/TheRightResolutionBook

2. http://www.books2read.com/TheCupidCaperBook

3. http://www.books2read.com/LuckyInLoveBook

4. http://www.books2read.com/MayIHaveThisDanceBook

5. http://www.books2read.com/FirstKissFireworksBook

6. http://www.books2read.com/FallingForeverThisTimeBook

7. http://www.books2read.com/ThankfulForLoveBook

8. http://www.books2read.com/MissionMistletoeBook

9. http://www.books2read.com/ShelterFromTheStorm

10. http://www.books2read.com/TheDoctorsUnexpectedFamily

73

Holiday of Hope[12]

Other Books by Kristen

Love Hallmark movies? Pick up Kristen's book October Kiss, based on the Hallmark movie viewers love! Available anywhere books are sold—in paperback, digital, and audio!
October Kiss from Hallmark Publishing[13]

---

11. http://www.books2read.com/HisTexasPrincess

12. http://www.books2read.com/HolidayOfHope

13. https://www.books2read.com/OctoberKiss

About Kristen

KRISTEN ETHRIDGE WRITES Sweet Escape Romance—stories with hope, heart and happily-ever-after—for Harlequin's Love Inspired line, Hallmark Publishing, and Laurel Lock Publishing. She's a Romance Writers of America Golden Heart Award nominee and both a Christian Fiction and Inspirational Romance #1 Best-Selling Author.

You can find Kristen in her native habitat—a Texas patio—where she's likely to be savoring the joy of a crispy taco, along with a glass of iced tea. Scents from her essential oil diffuser are also a must, since she's a certified aromatherapist. She's almost convinced her family that it's normal to talk to imaginary people, as long it goes in a book.

Find her online at http://www.kristenethridge.com where you can get a free story for signing up for her newsletter. You can also follow her adventures in writing at www.facebook.com/ kristenethridgebooks[1].

Keep up with Kristen by joining her newsletter list[2] and her author pages on Bookbub[3] and Facebook[4]. If you can't get enough of Port Provident, come join the Port Provident Community Center[5] on Facebook, the official gathering place for Kristen and her fans.

www.kristenethridge.com[6]

Facebook[7] Instagram[8]

The Port Provident Community[9] Center

Don't forget...if you love sweet escape romances, join Kristen's newsletter[10]!

---

1.   http://www.facebook.com/kristenethridgebooks

2.   http://www.kristenethridge.com/newsletter

3.   https://www.bookbub.com/authors/kristen-ethridge

4.   http://www.facebook.com/kristenethridgebooks

5.   https://www.facebook.com/groups/2422381554654795

6. http://www.kristenethridge.com

7. https://www.facebook.com/KristenEthridgeBooks

8. https://instagram.com/kristenethridge

9. https://www.facebook.com/groups/2422381554654795

10. http://www.kristenethridge.com

Acknowledgements

FOR THE PEOPLE WHO aren't afraid to talk about mental health so others don't feel so alone. For the people who stand in the gap and pray for those who hurt. For the people who find the hope deep inside every day to continue to search for the light to break through the fog.

LAUREL LOCK PUBLISHING

Publisher's Note: This is a work of fiction. Names, characters, places, and incidents are a product of the author's imagination. Locales and public names are sometimes used for atmospheric purposes. Any resemblance to actual people, living or dead, or to businesses, companies, events, institutions, or locales is completely coincidental.

Scriptures taken from the Holy Bible, New International Version®, NIV®. Copyright © 1973, 1978, 1984, 2011 by Biblica, Inc.™ Used by permission of Zondervan. All rights reserved worldwide. www.zondervan.com[1] The "NIV" and "New International Version" are trademarks registered in the United States Patent and Trademark Office by Biblica, Inc.™

Book Layout ©2013 BookDesignTemplates.com

www.ingramcontent.com/pod-product-compliance
Lightning Source LLC
Chambersburg PA
CBHW030356180626
46812CB00007B/2917